I WANT TO

WIND

WHAT MAKES YOU MOVE?

By Francesca Grazzini
illustrated by Chiara Carrer
Translated by Talia Wise

A CURIOUS NELL BOOK

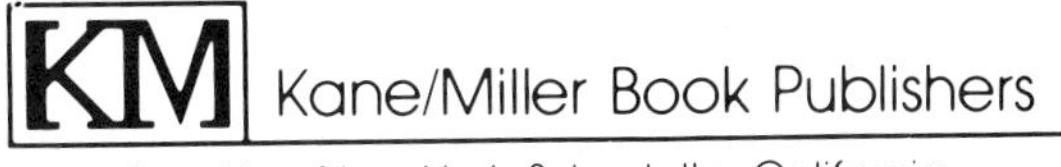

Brooklyn, New York & La Jolla, California

Please wind, don't
blow so hard!
Can't you see I'm
having trouble flying?

I’m much stronger
than you, little sparrow.
But, did you know I can
also be a help to birds?

When birds make long journeys
and get tired of flapping their wings,
I can carry them along.

What are you made of wind?

I am made of air,
which surrounds everything . . .

. . . not only in the sky,

. . . but everywhere!

But air doesn't move fast . . .

You're right,
air can be still
and calm, but . . .

. . . when it starts moving
quickly, it becomes wind.
This is great for kite flying!

I'll show you one way air starts moving quickly to become wind. First, you have to know that hot air loves to go up, taking the place of cold air as it rises.

That's why, if you are in a room and you climb a staircase, you will discover it's warmer at the top.

Then where does the cold air that was at the top go?

Good little sparrow!
You've asked a good question.
When there is too much air at the top, the extra air moves away to find a less crowded place.

The air that moves
away becomes wind.

Good little sparrow!

Wind, you seem so strong.

At certain times I'm stronger
than others. I get grades
for different strengths . . .
a bit like . . . school!

THE WIND'S REPORT CARD

GRADE 0
It's very calm

GRADE 3
Chimney smoke mo

GRADE 8
Trees sway to and fro

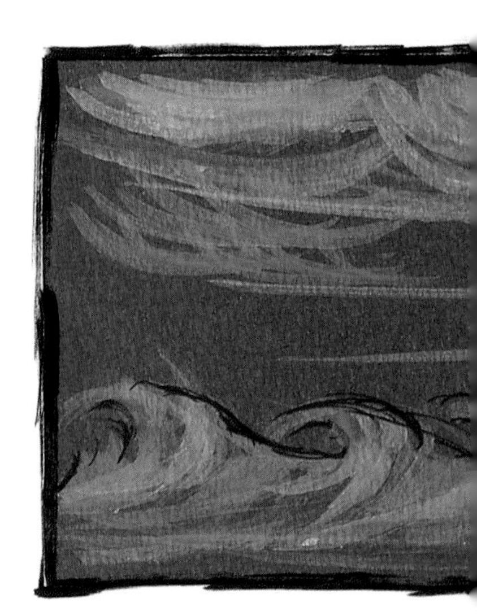

GRADE 10
There is a storm

GRADE 6
I move sail boats

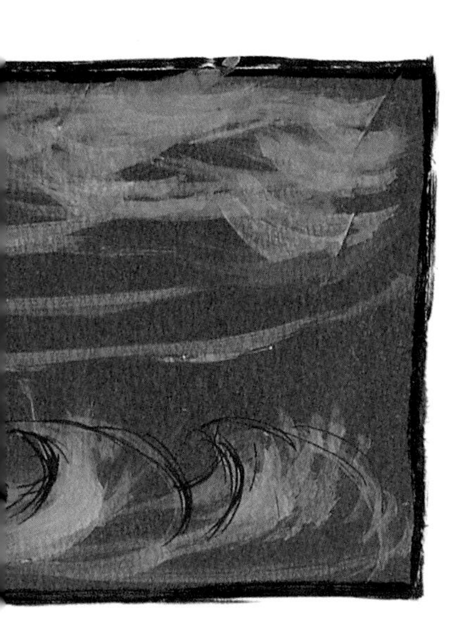

GRADE 12
There is a hurricane

THE WIND'S SONG

Up above the rooftops,
My weathervanes are turning
And over on the hillsides
My windmills keep on churning
To grind the wheat for flour
For pasta and for bread
To make crumbs for the little birds . . .
We've got to keep them fed!

I push the wind surfers and the
sail boats. . . . But do you know that
once I also pushed huge sailing ships?
In those days there weren't engines,
and when I stopped blowing, the sailing
ships had to stop.

WHEN THE WIND . . .

A hurricane is a very strong wind that sometimes lasts a day and sometimes a month and can destroy all things it finds in its path.

From a distance a tornado looks like a turned-over trumpet. It is made of a very strong wind that turns in circles around itself.

. . . BECOMES MEAN

A cyclone is made of wind that turns around in circles too. But in the middle, the air is calm. The quiet center is sometimes called the eye of the storm.

There are also tornadoes that come from the ocean. Like regular tornadoes they are made of very strong wind that turns around itself, but in this case, the wind sucks up water.

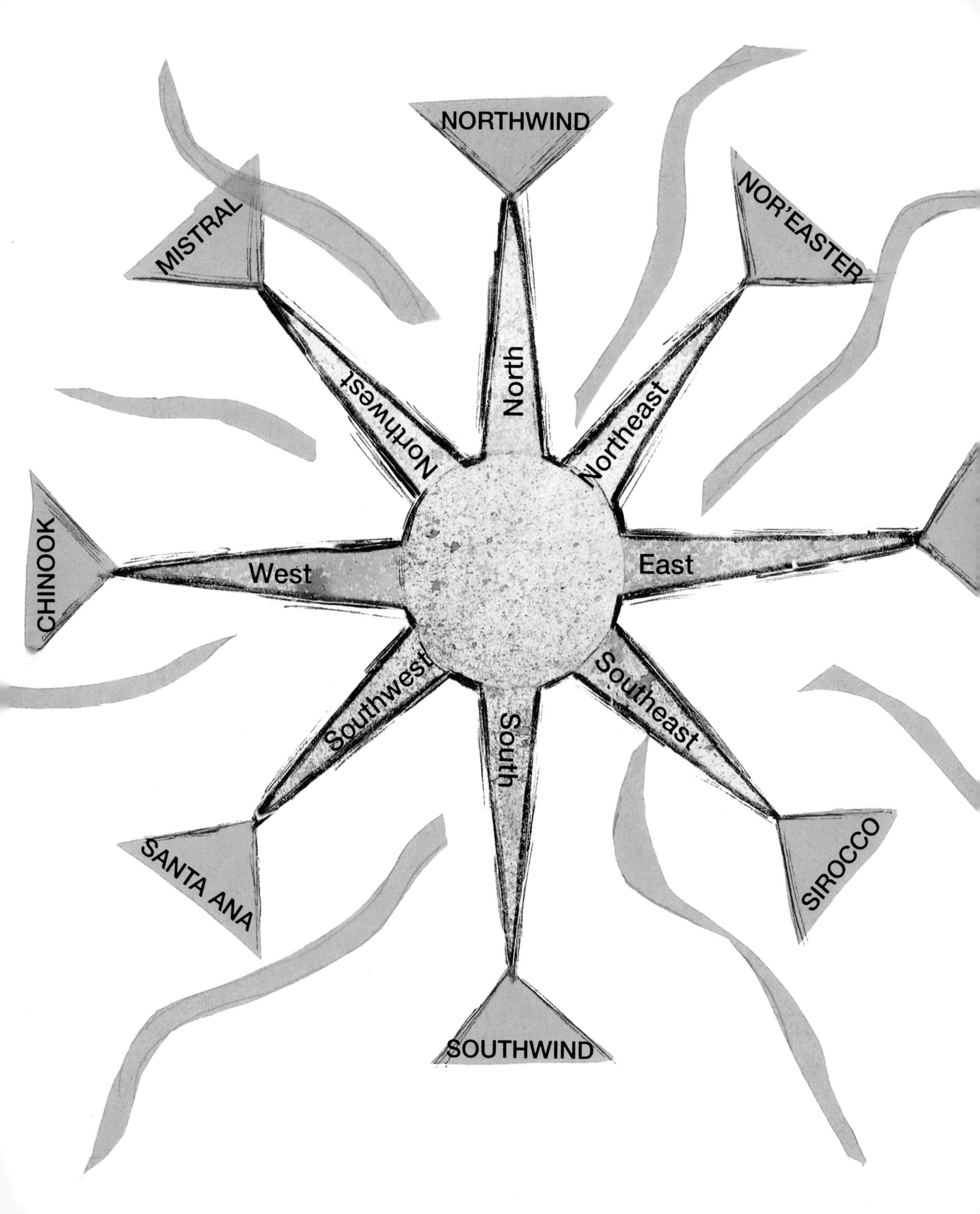
NORTHWIND
NOR'EASTER
MISTRAL
North
Northwest
Northeast
CHINOOK
West
East
Southwest
Southeast
South
SANTA ANA
SIROCCO
SOUTHWIND

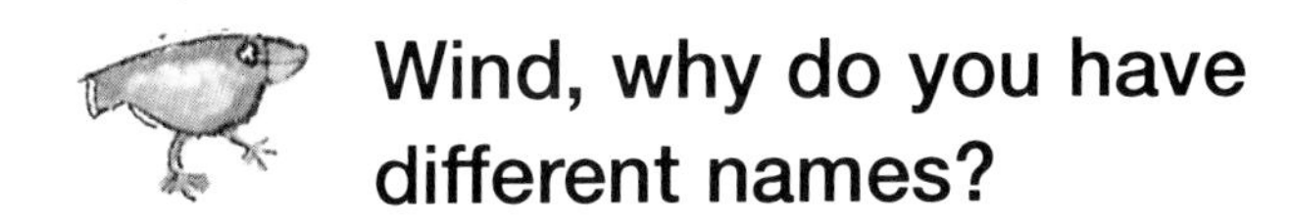

Wind, why do you have different names?

It depends on where I come from. If I come from the northeast, for example, I am very cold, and they call me a "Nor'easter". If I come from the southwest, I am warm and dry from crossing deserts, and they call me a "Santa Ana". But now I really have to go. Goodbye, little sparrow!

THE WIND . . .

Mary Poppins
is a magical nanny.
When she snaps her
fingers, toys go into their
places by themselves!
In the story, she arrives
in London gently carried
by the Eastwind . . .

. . . IN STORIES

In THE WIZARD OF OZ, Dorothy and her dog Toto are carried by a tornado that sucks up their house, taking it to the magical land of Oz. On the way to the Emerald City, they meet the Scarecrow, the Tin Man and the Cowardly Lion . . .

Do you know any other stories where wind is important?